The Rough Patch

Brian Lies

Greenwillow Books
An Imprint of HarperCollinsPublishers

For Laurel, partner and muse,
who always believed in this one

The Rough Patch
Text and illustrations copyright © 2018 by Brian Lies

All rights reserved. Printed in the United States of America.
For information address HarperCollins Children's Books,
a division of HarperCollins Publishers, 195 Broadway, New York, NY 10007.
www.harpercollinschildrens.com

The illustrations in this book were created with acrylics, oils, and colored pencils on Strathmore paper.
The text type is 26-point Venetian 301 BT.

Library of Congress Cataloging-in-Publication Data
Names: Lies, Brian, author, illustrator.
Title: The rough patch / written and illustrated by Brian Lies.
Description: First edition. | New York, NY : Greenwillow Books,
an imprint of HarperCollinsPublishers, [2018] |
Summary: Farmer Evan and his dog do everything together and, especially, in the garden but when his
dog passes away Evan lets his garden fill with weeds until a pumpkin vine brings new hope.
Identifiers: LCCN 2017034540 | ISBN 9780062671271 ((hardcover))
Subjects: | CYAC: Loss (Psychology)—Fiction. | Gardens—Fiction. | Dogs—Fiction. |
Farm life—Fiction.
Classification: LCC PZ7.L618 Rou 2018 | DDC [E]—dc23
LC record available at https://lccn.loc.gov/2017034540

19 20 21 22 PC 10 9 8 7 6 5 4
First Edition

Greenwillow Books

*E*van and his dog did everything together.

They played games
and enjoyed sweet treats.

They shared music
and adventure.

They were together
all through the day,
and through all the seasons.

But what they loved the most was
working in Evan's magnificent garden.

There, everything they planted grew as big

and as beautiful as the sky above them.

But one day, the unthinkable happened.

Evan laid his dog to rest in a corner of the garden,

and nothing was the same.

Evan shut himself away inside.

One morning, he found himself with
a hoe in his paws. Swinging angrily,
he slashed the garden to the ground.

He hacked it all to bits and threw everything into a heap.

But a good place won't stay empty for long.
New plants sprouted and stretched toward the sky.

Weeds.

Itchy ones.

Spiky and prickly ones.

Foul-smelling ones.

These weeds suited Evan just fine,

so he took care of them.

If Evan's garden couldn't be a happy place,
then it was going to be the saddest
and most desolate spot he could make it.

DO NOT
TOUCH

When Evan found a pumpkin vine sneaking
in under the fence, he raised his hoe to
chop it. But then he considered its prickly stems,
fuzzy leaves, and spidery, twisty tendrils.

He let it be.

As the pumpkin vine grew, Evan cleared the weeds from its path and watered it. The vine responded to his care.

Around the time the evening air began to cool,
Evan felt an old, familiar sense of excitement.

It was Fair Week.

He loaded up the pumpkin and drove to town.

He took care of
important fair business,

and gobbled down
some delicious fair food.

He caught up with some friends,
too. It felt good to be out again,
even if it wasn't quite the same.

Evan's pumpkin won third place.

"Prize is ten dollars or one of the pups in that box," the judge said.

"I'll take the ten," said Evan.

But as he claimed his prize,
he heard a scrabbling sound inside the box
and thought it wouldn't hurt

to just . . .

look.